From Beans to Batteries

By Steve Brace ◆ Illustrated by Annie Kubler

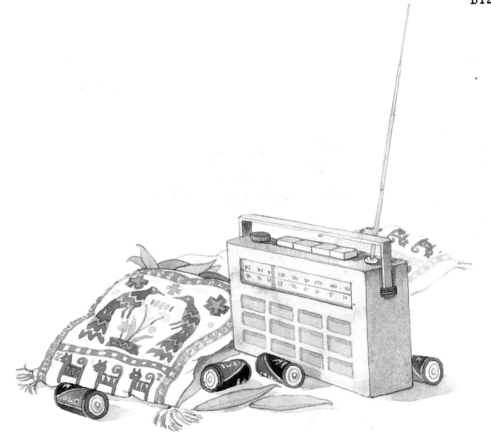

Published by Child's Play (International) Ltd
Swindon   Auburn   Sydney   St. Catharines
© 1998 Child's Play®   ISBN 0-85953-799-4   Printed in China
A catalogue reference for this book is available from the British Library

Aldomaro lives in a village
called Pampagrande,
high in the Andes
mountains in Peru.

Whenever he can,
he likes to listen
to the radio.

Aldomaro has been working in the fields.

He hurries home to listen to
Dr. Manami's Half Hour.

For someone, like Aldomaro,
who wants to be a doctor,
it is very informative.

Oh, dear!
Something is wrong.
The radio doesn't work.

Señor Antonio, Aldomaro's father,
is sorting potatoes.

**"Sorry, Aldomaro. I can't
spare the time to look at it now."**

Aldomaro runs to his mother.

"Don't worry, dear. It's only the batteries," she says.

"Please, may we go to Bambamarca to buy some?"

"Yes, chiquito. But you will have to sell some beans in the market to pay for them. Ask Amerita to help you."

The batteries will cost about one sol.

Aldomaro and his sister
pick a kilo of beans.
That should be enough.

It is a three hour walk
to the market in Bambamarca.

**"Make sure you are
home before dark,"**
mother urges.

The first person they meet is Uncle Pablo. He has been working since daybreak.

"We're going to market, Uncle Pablo."

"Hello, Amerita. Hello, little Doctor.
I wish I could come with you."

Everybody knows that Aldomaro
wants to be a doctor.

In the next village, a new school
is being built by the villagers.

They meet their teacher, Maria.
She teaches art, science and Spanish
in their school.

"Good afternoon, Señorita Maria."
"Good afternoon, children."

"Don't go so fast, Amerita.
If I spill the beans,
we won't be able to sell them.
Then we won't be able to buy batteries."

At last, Bambamarca is in sight.

"Phew! I need a rest," says Amerita.

"Me, too!" says Aldomaro.

From high above the town,
they see the bustling streets.

**"Look, Aldomaro.
There's the cattle market.
Let's hurry."**

"Selling cattle looks easy,
but who will buy our beans?"

The children reach the main market.

**"Will you buy our beans,
Señorita?"**

"Not today, my dears."

"Please, Señor.
Will you give us
one sol
for our beans?"

"I don't like beans."

At the hat stall,
the children cheer up.

**"You look silly,
Amerita."**

**"Not as silly
as you!"**

At the fabric stall,
there's more bad news.

**"I'll give you one half sol,
and not one centavo more."**

**"Thank you, Señor.
We are sorry, but
it's not enough."**

The hardware stall is closing.

"Even if we sell our beans, we'll never be able to buy our batteries now."

"And I won't be able to hear *Dr. Manami's Half Hour.*"

The kindly old stall-holder
has overheard the children.

"My wife told me
to bring home
some beans for dinner
and I forgot.
She will be furious.
PLEASE, will you
sell me yours?

"And while you
are listening
to your broadcast,
I'll be enjoying
a delicious bean stew.
What a bargain!"

SUCCESS!

Aldomaro and Amerita set off
for home to Pampagrande.
Listening to their radio makes
the journey seem much shorter.

Aldomaro wants to be a doctor.
What do you want to be?
What do you use batteries for?
If you needed batteries, what would you do?
How far would you have to go to buy some?

Where does Aldomaro live?
Can you find his home on the map?
Would you like to live there?
Or visit him?
Would Aldomaro like to visit you?
What would he most enjoy?
What would he miss from his village?